The Aliens Who Loved Lemon Curd

Written by

Lorraine Piddington

Illustrated by Jacqueline Tee

Grosvenor House
Publishing Limited

This book is published by
Grosvenor House Publishing Ltd
28-30 High Street, Guildford, Surrey, GU1 3HY.
www.grosvenorhousepublishing.co.uk

A CIP record for this book
is available from the British Library

ISBN 978-1-78623-810-8

For Claire, Lee, Carly and Zachary

The aliens who loved lemon curd
Were really loud and quite absurd.

They arrived in their spaceship by chance one day
Saw some lemon curd and decided to stay.

They ate it greedily by the jar
And gathered supplies from near and far.

Soon the shops had empty shelves

They'd taken it all for themselves!

The aliens' demand became too great
The more they bought the more they ate!

People tried to tempt them with jars of honey
But the aliens were fast running out of money.

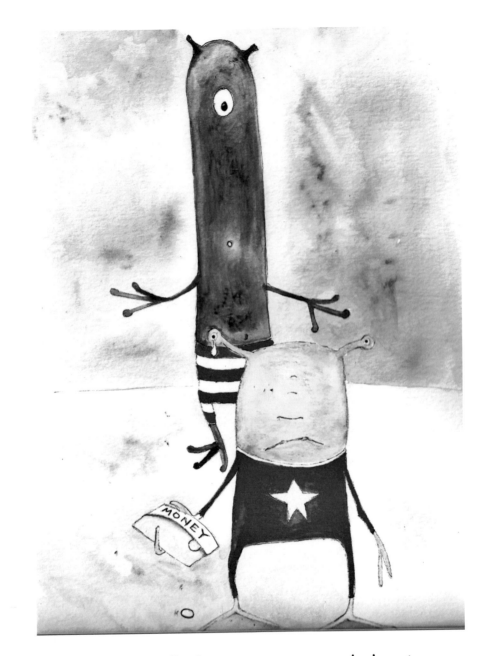

They sadly began to cry and shout

"Our money has nearly all run out!"

"On our planet spiders are used."

But the shopkeepers were not amused.

The spiders escaped and went everywhere

The shop assistants began to scream and stare!

"You can't pay with spiders!" they would say.

While others would shout and run away

"Everyone loves spiders!" said the alien queen,

"We feed them on flies in bowls of ice cream."

You can't use spiders to pay for food
It's not allowed and would be rude!

On planet Earth you need money

Pockets full of spiders just aren't funny!

The alien queen was wise and old

And said, "I declare my treasure must be sold!"

"We need to pay for the things we like,
And I would love a new blue bike!"

So all the aliens put their spiders away,

To save them for a rainy day.

Then everyone ate their favourite treat
That is yellow sticky and lemony sweet.

Lemon curd on toast, with carrots or cheese
The aliens loved all of these,

So if you have luscious lemon curd
Eat it quietly so you can't be heard.

Then lock it away where the aliens can't see
And shh! Don't tell anyone where you hide the key.

Lightning Source UK Ltd.
Milton Keynes UK
UKRC01n1123220117
292561UK00006B/50